THE GHOST AT CAMP DAVID

by **Ron Roy**
illustrated by **Timothy Bush**

A STEPPING STONE BOOK™

Random House 🏠 New York

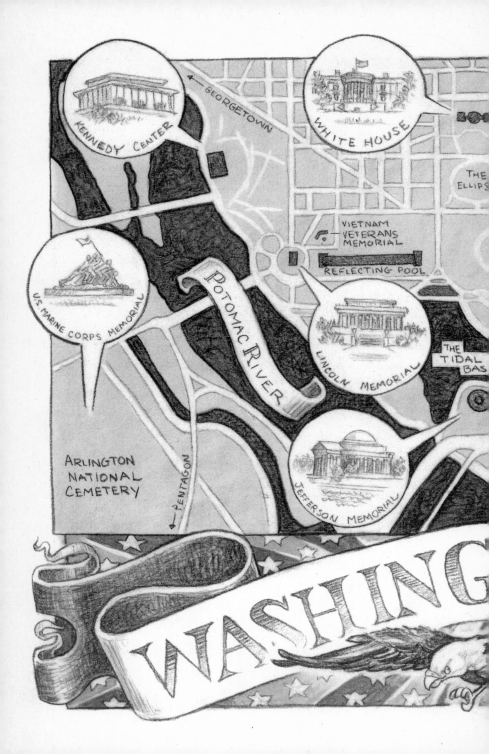

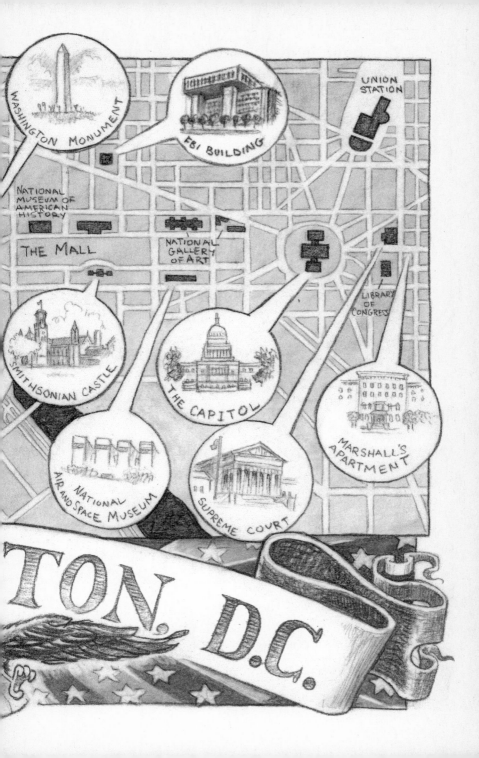

This book is dedicated to my readers.
—R.R.

Photo credits: pp. 88–89, courtesy of the National Archives.

Published in the United States by Random House Children's Books, a division of Random House, Inc., New York.

Random House and the colophon are registered trademarks and A Stepping Stone Book and the colophon are trademarks of Random House, Inc.

Visit us on the Web!
www.steppingstonesbooks.com
www.randomhouse.com/kids

Educators and librarians, for a variety of teaching tools, visit us at
www.randomhouse.com/teachers

Library of Congress Cataloging-in-Publication Data
Roy, Ron.
The ghost at Camp David / by Ron Roy ; illustrated by Timothy Bush. — 1st ed.
p.   cm. — (Capital mysteries ; 12)
"A Stepping Stone Book."
Summary: KC and her friend Marshall accompany KC's stepfather, the United States President, to remote Camp David, where they find clues that point to either ghostly or criminal activity.
ISBN 978-0-375-85925-0 (pbk.) — ISBN 978-0-375-95925-7 (lib. bdg.)
[1. Robbers and outlaws—Fiction. 2. Ghosts—Fiction. 3. Camp David (Md.)—Fiction. 4. Presidents—Fiction. 5. Mystery and detective stories.]
I. Bush, Timothy, ill. II. Title.
PZ7.R8139Gho 2010   [Fic]—dc22   2009026425

Printed in the United States of America
10 9 8 7 6 5 4 3 2 1

Contents

1. The Deer in the Fog   1

2. The Lonely Little Cabin   6

3. The Strange Red Stain   16

4. Mud or Blood?   23

5. Noises in the Night   35

6. Mysterious Visitor   47

7. What's Under the Floor?   55

8. Trapdoor   64

9. A Face at the Window   72

10. Marshall and the Mole People   81

1

The Deer in the Fog

KC and Marshall hurried through the White House gate. It was three o'clock on Friday afternoon, October 14. School was out, and the kids were going to Camp David with the president for the weekend.

"Are we really taking the helicopter?" Marshall asked.

"Yup," KC said. "My stepdad said it will only take half an hour to get there."

Both kids had packed the night before. Their duffel bags were already in the president's helicopter.

KC and Marshall ran across the White House lawn. Two marines stood at attention next to the helicopter. They gave

KC and Marshall a boost up into the passenger compartment.

President Thornton was sitting next to his pilot. "Hi there," the president greeted KC and Marshall. "How was school?"

"We had science, and it was great," Marshall said. "We learned why leaves turn different colors in the autumn."

"And this March we're gonna go to a place where they make maple syrup," KC added.

"There are plenty of maple trees at Camp David," the president said. "Maybe we can try making syrup this spring!"

"Cool!" Marshall said.

"Okay, buckle up, you guys," the president said. He clicked his seat belt shut.

KC and Marshall buckled themselves into their seats.

"You can take off now, Jeff," the president said to the pilot.

"Yes, sir!" Jeff said. The copter lifted into the air. KC and Marshall waved at the marines down below. They waved back as Jeff turned the chopper into the clouds.

"Where is Camp David, anyway?" asked Marshall. He had to shout to be heard over the noise of the helicopter.

"In Thurmont, Maryland!" KC yelled back.

The president turned around. "Camp David is in the Catoctin Mountains," he explained. "If we're lucky, we'll see some wildlife. There are plenty of deer, bobcats, and a few bears."

"I wish Mom could have come," KC said. Her mother, the First Lady, had gone to Florida to visit KC's aunt.

"You'll have lots of stories to tell her when she gets back," the president said.

About thirty minutes later, the helicopter hovered over a thick, dark forest. Fog covered the trees, making it hard to see the ground.

"Gee, how can we land with all this fog?" Marshall asked KC. He had his nose mashed against his window.

KC didn't answer. She was watching the fog swirl over the tops of the trees. She thought it looked like flying ghosts.

"There's the camp," the president said, pointing.

KC's breath was fogging the window. She wiped it clean. She could just make out a few buildings through the fog and the blue water of a swimming pool. A tall fence wound among the trees.

"Taking her down, sir," Jeff said to the president.

KC and Marshall watched the ground get closer. The wind from the helicopter blades blew the fog around and bent the tree branches.

Just before they landed, a deer bounded from a clump of bushes. "Look!" KC shouted. "A deer!"

"Where?" Marshall asked. He leaned across KC to look out her window. "All I see is fog!"

Then KC spotted something else—or thought she did. Something the color of fog was scurrying between the trees. She couldn't tell if it was a human or a wild animal. She wiped her breath from the window and looked again. The thing had disappeared.

2

The Lonely Little Cabin

Jeff helped the president and the kids step to the ground. He handed a heavy briefcase to the president. KC knew it was filled with books, files, and a laptop. The president had told her he had a lot of work to do that weekend.

"Here you go, kids," Jeff said. He gave them their duffel bags.

"Thanks, Jeff," the president said. He was shouting over the noise of the helicopter blades. "Have a good flight back."

The president led KC and Marshall away as the helicopter rose, then vanished into the fog.

KC looked around. They were in a

grassy clearing. Through the fog, she saw what looked like a guard's hut near the fence. Two marines stood near the hut. Then she saw a shed near a grove of trees. The shed door opened and a man jogged toward them.

"That's Gus," the president said. "He's the caretaker here."

Gus and the president shook hands. "Gus, this is my stepdaughter, KC, and her friend Marshall."

KC glanced at Gus's green overalls. Had he been what she saw from the helicopter?

"We didn't expect you this weekend, sir," Gus said.

"I know," said the president. "Sorry about the short notice."

"It's fine, sir. Always a pleasure!" Gus

said. "Aspen Lodge is all ready for you."

"Who's Aspen Lodge?" KC asked.

The president chuckled. "That's the name of the cabin presidents always stay in," he said. "There are a lot of smaller cabins for guests. Each one is named after a different kind of tree or plant."

Gus led them to a small golf cart. He climbed into the driver's seat. "Hop in!" he said.

Gus turned a key, and the golf cart lurched forward. It putt-putted along a gravel road lined by trees. Most of the leaves had turned red and gold.

Parked between two small cabins was a white van with the words WHITE'S LAUNDRY SERVICE on the side. Not far away was another guard hut. KC had read that Camp David security was especially tight when the president was visiting.

After a few minutes, Gus pulled the golf cart up in front of a large building. It had two floors, a lot of windows, and a tall chimney. A sign near the front door said ASPEN.

"Here we are, sir," Gus said. He looked at the sky. "Storm coming, I'll bet."

"I think you're right," the president said. "But we'll be cozy and dry inside Aspen."

After KC, Marshall, and the president hopped out, Gus left with a wave.

The door to Aspen opened. A woman in a black dress and white apron stepped out. She had dark hair and a round face. "Welcome, Mr. President," she said. "I'm Anna. Florence is sick, so I'm filling in for her. She had to stay home."

The president shook hands with Anna. "I hope it isn't serious," he said.

"Just a bad cold," Anna told them. "Please, come in. I already lit a fire and made a snack."

"Thank you, Anna." The president led the way to the large living room. On one wall, a fire crackled in a stone fireplace. Filled bookcases and display cases ran along the other walls. KC counted three sofas and at least ten big chairs.

"This place is awesome!" Marshall said.

KC walked over to a long window. "Hey, Marsh, there's the pool I saw from the helicopter," she said. "Too bad it's too cold for swimming."

KC thought the pool looked spooky with fog over the water. Then she noticed a tiny cabin not far from the pool. It resembled the cottages she'd seen in fairy-tale books when she was little.

KC grabbed the president's hand. She pulled him over to the window. "Can Marshall and I sleep in that little cabin?" she asked. "It's so cute!"

"Sure, I guess so," the president said. He looked at Anna. "Can you get someone to make up the beds?"

"Sir, there's only the one bed and the sofa," Anna said. "I'm afraid it's a bit dirty, too. No one uses Witch Hazel."

"The cabin is called *Witch Hazel*?" Marshall squawked. He peeked out the window. "It looks like a witch lives in it!"

The president laughed. "Witch hazel is the name of a tree," he explained. "Come on. While Anna gets Witch Hazel ready, I'll show you around Aspen."

Everywhere they looked were photographs of past presidents and world leaders. In the center of the dining room stood a gleaming wooden table and twelve chairs. There was another fireplace in the corner.

KC stopped in front of a glass case at least ten feet long. Inside were shelves of silver cups, bowls, and candlestick holders. The silver was polished to a glow and looked old and expensive.

"What's this for?" KC asked.

"Those are gifts left here by other presidents," her stepfather said. "Each president leaves a piece of silver as a gift. There are pieces from Franklin Roosevelt, Eisenhower, Nixon, and the Bush family. Your mom and I bought that bowl." He pointed. "See my name on it?"

"What about George Washington?" Marshall asked.

"The first president to stay here was Franklin Roosevelt in 1942," the president explained. "When Washington was president, Native Americans lived in this area."

The president leaned in closer to KC and Marshall. "There's a legend that says the ghosts of all those old presidents come back to visit," he said in a low voice.

"You're teasing us!" KC said.

"Nope. It's true. On their birthdays, the presidents' ghosts come and wander around the camp, peeking in windows." He winked at Anna, who had returned with a tray of snacks. "On warm nights, they even splash in the pool!"

Marshall made a face. "They better not peek in my window!"

Hearing the ghost story made KC remember the figure she'd seen through the fog. "I saw something running just before we landed," she said. "I saw a deer, too, then this other thing. I'm not even sure it was a person."

"It could have been almost anything," the president said. "A lot of deer live here inside our security fences. It may have been a coyote. Sometimes they sneak under the fences or through the gates."

"Great!" Marshall yelped. "Ghosts and coyotes and witches! Can I call my mom and go home?"

3

The Strange Red Stain

Anna put a plate of cookies, a pitcher of milk, and three glasses on the table.

"Thank you, Anna," the president said as she left the room.

KC was flipping through a large book. "Look, Marsh," she said. "This tells about all the presidents who used to come to Camp David."

Marshall grabbed a cookie and dunked it in his milk. "Is your picture in it?" he asked KC's stepfather.

"Not yet," the president said, sipping his milk.

"Guys," KC said, "it says here that today is President Eisenhower's birthday!

He was born on October 14, 1890."

The president grinned. "That means his ghost may be visiting us tonight."

KC showed Marshall and the president a picture in the book.

"Why is he wearing an army uniform?" asked Marshall.

"He was a general before he became our thirty-fourth president," President Thornton explained.

"When was he president?" KC asked.

"From 1953 to 1961," her stepfather said. "Two terms. In fact, he named Camp David after his grandson, David Eisenhower. David was about your age when he first came here with his grandfather."

"Don't tell me he's dead, too," Marshall groaned. "This place will be crawling with ghosts!"

"Don't worry," the president said. "David is alive and well."

Anna came back into the room. "The cabin is ready," she said.

They left the cookies and followed her out the back door. KC and Marshall carried their duffel bags. Anna led them along a stone path past the pool. The clouds had turned darker, and a strong wind blew through the trees. The tiny cabin looked lonely.

"Are you sure you want to stay here by yourselves?" the president asked.

"It'll be fun!" KC said. "We can pretend we're Hansel and Gretel!"

"Oh, great," Marshall said. "Didn't a witch try to cook them?"

Anna opened the door. KC stepped inside first. They were in a small room with dark green walls. A round rug covered most of the floor. There was one sofa and one chair. A wooden trunk sat near the sofa. Pictures of birds and flowers hung on the walls. The window looked out at the back of Aspen Lodge.

Between the living room and bedroom was a bathroom. KC peeked in and saw fluffy towels on a rack. A pile of paper hand towels sat on the sink.

"I like it!" KC said.

Marshall stuck his head in the bedroom. Someone had made the bed and turned on a lamp. There was one small window. "This place was built for little forest creatures," he muttered. "It even smells like a cave."

KC sniffed the air. "That's just nature you smell," she said. She dropped her bag on the sofa. "This is where I'm sleeping."

Marshall tossed his bag onto the bed in the next room.

"Well, I need to do some work," the president said. "Come over to Aspen later."

"Can we go exploring before it rains?" KC asked.

"Sure, just don't get lost," the president said. "There are two hundred acres of woods here."

The president and Anna left. KC switched on the lamp near the sofa. She unzipped her backpack and dumped everything onto the rug.

"You brought books?" Marshall asked.

KC laughed. "Duh, we have homework, remember?"

"Oh yeah," Marshall groaned.

KC had also brought her Swiss Army

knife and a flashlight, plus some jeans, a sweatshirt, and pajamas. "I can keep my stuff in this little trunk," she said.

KC opened the trunk's lid. It was empty except for some dirt on the bottom. She wet a few paper towels at the bathroom sink and wiped the inside of the chest.

The paper towel turned red. "Yuck!" KC said.

"What did you find? A spider?" asked Marshall. "Let me see!" Marshall got along with all kinds of animals. He especially liked spiders.

"No spiders," KC said. "Just some red dirt." She took the towels into the bathroom and dropped them in the trash can.

Marshall let out a spooky laugh and made his eyes cross. "No, it's not red dirt, little girl," he whispered. "It's *bloooood*!"

4
Mud or Blood?

"Ha-ha. Very funny, Marsh," KC said. "Maybe it's blood from Hazel the witch!"

Marshall laughed. "Stop, or I'll have nightmares!"

"You started it," KC said. She dumped her stuff into the trunk and closed the lid. She set her books and a notebook on the top. "Let's go exploring."

Marshall looked out the window. "It's gonna rain pretty soon," he said.

"We can run back when it starts," KC said as she opened the door.

The kids passed Aspen Lodge. A few lights were on, glowing softly through the fog. Soon they came to the swimming pool.

It was surrounded by a fence with a locked gate. Red and yellow leaves floated on the water.

A bat flew low over their heads. "Yikes!" KC said, ducking. The bat zoomed between Aspen Lodge, Witch Hazel cabin, and the pool.

"Is it drinking or looking for mosquitoes?" KC asked.

"I don't know," Marshall said. He lowered his voice. "Maybe it's a vampire, looking for you!"

More bats flitted overhead. "The bats sure like it here," KC said.

She and Marshall started walking again, but a minute later, KC stopped.

"Hey, Marsh, look!" she said. She was standing next to a post with a sign on it. The sign said NANCY'S WALK.

"Who's Nancy?" Marshall asked.

"I don't know," KC said. "It looks like a nature trail. Come on."

The kids turned right, heading away from Aspen Lodge. The trail was covered in leaves and pine needles. Small labels named some of the trees. They crossed a narrow wooden bridge over a stream. Their feet made clunking sounds.

"Isn't this cool?" KC asked. "Think how many presidents have hiked along this exact path!"

Just then thunder rumbled somewhere in the distance.

"I'll bet none of them were dumb enough to do it in a thunderstorm!" said Marshall.

"It's only thunder," KC said. "Let's keep going."

KC and Marshall hiked further. KC spotted a tree with bright red leaves. She picked a handful of the leaves and slipped them into her jacket pocket.

Marshall read the small sign next to the tree. "It's called a swamp maple," he said. "Excellent, KC, we're hiking through a swamp! There could be alligators watching us, licking their lips!"

KC laughed at her friend. "Alligators don't hang out in Maryland," she said. "And they don't have lips!"

A few yards along, the trail bent around a giant pine tree. When the kids followed the trail, KC noticed a tall iron fence on one side. The fence ran in both directions, through the fog and the trees.

KC went over to a pile of dirt near the fence. She looked around for a hole but

didn't see one. "I wonder why this dirt is here," she said to Marshall.

"Some animal dug a burrow," Marshall said.

KC shook her head. "I thought so, too, but there's no hole. And look, another pile of dirt over there."

"Good evening, Miss Corcoran, Mr. Li," a deep voice said.

KC and Marshall both jumped and turned around. A tall marine was standing near the pine tree. He glanced up at the sky. "You'd better head back to Aspen soon," he said.

"How did you know our names?" Marshall asked.

"I know everything about President Thornton," the guard said. "Don't get wet." The marine disappeared into the fog.

"Wow, he scared me," Marshall whispered. "What's he doing wandering around in the woods?"

"Security, Marsh," KC said. "The president told me they have patrols watching this place all the time."

"Well, I wish they wouldn't just pop up and give people heart attacks," Marshall said.

"He's right, we should head back," KC said. "I just felt a raindrop."

A bolt of lightning lit the sky in a streak. Thunder followed.

"Race you!" KC said. She took off running, with Marshall on her heels.

Marshall stopped when he got to the wooden bridge. Rain was falling faster now, splashing in the stream. The wooden railing felt slick under his fingers.

KC was nowhere to be seen.

"Okay, KC, where are you?" Marshall called out.

"Right behind you, licking my big, fat alligator lips!" KC yelled. She jumped out from behind a bush.

"Very funny," Marshall said. "It would serve you right if that was poison ivy. Come on, I'm getting soaked!"

They ran along Nancy's Walk until they came to Aspen Lodge. Behind Aspen, Witch Hazel looked sad and wet. The kids cut across some lawn to their cabin. Lights were on in both rooms.

KC and Marshall grabbed towels and wiped their hair and faces.

KC pulled the leaves she'd collected from her jacket pocket. "I'm going to press these," she said. She opened her notebook and placed the leaves between the pages.

"Hey, check your feet," Marshall called from his room. "My sneakers are pretty muddy."

KC looked at the soles of her sneakers. "Mine too," she said.

There were chunks of mud on the floor and rug. She took her sneakers off and went into the bathroom to get some paper towels.

Marshall came in, carrying his sneakers. "It's probably from those dirt piles in the woods," he said.

KC wiped her sneakers as clean as she could get them. When she dropped the towels into the trash can, she noticed something. "Look," she said. "The mud on our sneakers is like the red dirt I wiped from inside that little trunk."

Marshall grabbed some towels to wipe his own sneakers. "So?"

"Nothing. I'm just wondering what red mud is doing inside that chest," KC said. "Especially since Anna told us no one uses this cabin."

Marshall compared the red stains on both paper towels. "It does look like the same stuff," he said.

KC tossed the towels away. "Let's go next door," she said. She went to put her sneakers back on.

"Wait a sec while I wash my hands," Marshall said.

Suddenly Marshall popped his head out of the bathroom. His hands were dripping water.

"I heard something!" he said with big eyes.

KC rolled her eyes. "Let me guess, it's an alligator or a witch, right?"

"No, I'm serious!" Marshall said. "It was like a knocking noise." He pointed to the floor. "I think it came from down there!"

Marshall shut off the water. They stood still and listened. Then they both heard a muffled noise coming from beneath their feet.

5

Noises in the Night

"I know what that is," KC said, leaving the bathroom. "When you don't run water for a long time, the pipes can make noises. That used to happen in our apartment before we moved into the White House."

Marshall wiped his hands and left the bathroom. Suddenly he grinned at KC. "You don't suppose it's President Eisenhower's ghost, do you?"

"Living in the bathroom pipes? I don't think so!" KC said.

"But ghosts can hide anywhere!" said Marshall. He gave a tug on KC's long, damp curls. "Even in your hair!"

"Or inside your bed covers!" KC said.

She opened the door and they ran through the rain to Aspen. The president was sitting at a small table near the fireplace. Books, papers, and his laptop were spread out in front of him. He looked up when the kids entered.

"You guys look a little damp," he said. "Find anything interesting in the woods?"

"I got some pretty leaves," KC said. "And we found Nancy's Walk. Who's Nancy?"

The president rubbed his eyes. "That's Nancy Reagan. When her husband was president, they made a lot of changes to Camp David. They fixed up Aspen Lodge to make it more comfortable. They both liked to hike, so they created that nature trail. President Reagan named it for his wife."

Thunder crashed over the house.

Raindrops smacked the windows and exploded across the glass.

"Boy, what a storm," the president said. He looked at his watch. "Dinner should be about ready. Want to check?"

The dining room table had been set for three. Anna brought in a platter of spaghetti and meatballs. Next came a tray of garlic bread and a bowl of salad.

"This looks and smells wonderful," the president said. "Thanks, Anna."

"No trouble at all, sir," Anna said. "I'll be in Florence's room if you need me. I'm sleeping there tonight." She walked down a hallway toward the back of the building. A flash of lightning lit up the windows.

"There's plenty of room here in Aspen if you kids change your minds," the president said.

"No thanks. We like our little cabin," KC said. "Right, Marsh?"

Before Marshall could answer, Anna returned. "The phone in Florence's room isn't working," she said. She picked up the living room phone and shook her head. "The storm must have done some damage."

"Thanks, Anna," the president said. "I'm sure Gus and the staff will get it all fixed up. Besides, I have my cell phone."

With a nod, Anna left the room, and KC, Marshall, and the president began filling their plates.

Suddenly they heard three knocks.

"Did you hear something?" Marshall asked.

"I heard knocking," KC said.

"Maybe it's Gus," the president said.

He went to the door. No one was there. A wind gust blew rainwater over his feet.

The president sat down. "Ghosts, I guess," he said with a little smile.

Then KC heard more knocks. She looked at Marshall. "I know it's you!" she said. "You're bumping the bottom of the table with your knee!"

Marshall burst out laughing. "You should have seen your face," he said.

KC grinned. "Was that you in the bathroom before?" she asked. "Did you fake those noises, too?"

Marshall had a full mouth. He shook his head.

"What noises?" the president asked.

KC told the president about the sounds they had both heard under the bathroom floor.

"Marsh thought it was a ghost under the cabin," KC said.

The president winked at Marshall. "Well, it *is* President Eisenhower's birthday," he said.

"I said the pipes made those noises because the water hadn't been turned on for a long time," KC added.

"I'm sure you're right," the president said. "But there are tunnels under parts of Camp David." He pointed his fork down toward the floor. "Under this building, too."

"Are you teasing?" KC asked.

The president shook his head. "Nope. Cross my heart. There's a long tunnel leading to the other side of the security fence," he said. "In case the president ever has to leave Camp David fast."

"Sweet!" Marshall said. "Have you ever been down in the tunnel?"

"Only once," the president said. "It has a sort of safe room with food and fresh water, clothing, even beds. Thank goodness no president has ever had to use it."

"Can we see it?" KC asked.

"Sorry, it's top secret. Only a few people know there's such a tunnel, and how to get to it from this building," the president said.

KC and Marshall glanced around the large dining room. "Is there like a secret door or something?" KC asked.

The president nodded. "Very secret," he said.

They ate in silence for a few minutes.

"I made apple pie for dessert, sir," Anna said.

KC nearly jumped. She hadn't noticed Anna enter the room.

"I'll save mine till a little later," the president told her. "I don't know about these two, but I'm stuffed."

"I still have room!" Marshall said.

"Not me," KC said. "I'll have my pie tomorrow, Anna."

"And I've got a lot more reading to do," the president said. He folded his napkin. "Marshall, do you want to take your pie with you over to Witch Hazel?"

"Great idea!" Marshall said.

Anna wrapped Marshall's pie with a napkin and gave him a fork.

"You sure you want to sleep over there?" the president asked. "Not afraid of things under the floor?"

KC laughed. "I'll sleep all night long

while Marsh is hearing strange noises!" she said.

KC found a large blue umbrella in a stand by the door. It kept her and Marshall dry as they darted across the wet lawn to their cabin. By the sofa were pillows, sheets, and blankets.

"Anna must have done this," KC said. She flopped onto the sofa.

"Did she open the window, too?" Marshall asked. The only window in the small room was wide open. He walked over and shut it.

"Why would she open a window when it's raining?" KC asked.

Marshall wandered into his bedroom. "My window is open, too!"

"Maybe she wanted to air out the cabin," KC said.

Marshall slammed his window shut, then sat next to KC and began eating his pie.

Suddenly something black swooped down from the ceiling, nearly hitting Marshall's head.

"Duck!" Marshall yelled. "It's a pterodactyl!"

KC dived for the floor. She peeked up as the black thing flashed by again. "No, it's just another bat!" she said.

The kids watched the bat do a few more turns around the room.

KC jumped up and opened the door, letting rain blow in.

"What're you doing?" Marshall asked. "More bats will come in!"

"No, they won't," KC said. "They don't like humans." She ran into the bathroom and grabbed a towel. She chased the bat

around until it finally darted through the door and disappeared. KC closed the door.

"Lock it!" Marshall said.

"There's no lock," KC said. She grinned at Marshall, who was huddled on the floor. "Maybe the bat was after your pie."

Marshall swallowed the last bite. "Too late," he said.

The kids brushed their teeth and said good night. They each shut off their light.

Ten minutes after they'd gone to bed, KC sat up. She thought she'd heard something. Yes, there it was again. Knocking noises were coming from under the floor.

Those pipes again, she told herself. What else could it be?

6

Mysterious Visitor

KC slept snuggled in blankets on the sofa. She was having a dream about paddling a canoe on a quiet stream. Suddenly the stream became a rushing river. She dropped her paddle. The canoe was out of control, racing wildly down the river. It struck a rock, and that's when KC woke up.

It took a moment for KC to remember that she was safe in Witch Hazel cabin. Safe and dry, with her friend in the bedroom and her stepdad right next door.

KC's watch showed that it was nearly midnight. Outside, wind and rain lashed the cabin. She closed her eyes and went back to sleep.

But not for long. She felt a cool breeze. She heard something thump. Was she back in her dream? Back in the runaway canoe?

KC opened her eyes. A dark figure was kneeling in front of the chest where she had put her stuff. Suddenly the figure stood up, glanced at the sofa, and ran out the door. It slammed shut.

KC rubbed her eyes. Was that real? Or was she still dreaming? She turned on the light.

"KC? What's going on?"

Marshall was standing next to the sofa in Spider-Man pajamas. His hair looked like hamsters lived in it.

"Did you see him?" KC asked.

"See who?" Marshall asked.

KC pointed toward the door. "A guy, or maybe a woman, was standing in here," she said. "He was bent over this chest. Look, he put my books on the floor!"

KC jumped off the sofa and opened the chest. "Well, he didn't take anything," she said.

Marshall sat on the sofa. "What guy? What are you talking about?"

KC sat down next to him. "I was having this dream," she said. "I was in a canoe and lost my paddle. The canoe was going really fast, and I hit a rock, then I woke up."

She looked at Marshall. "And that's when I saw this . . . person. Then he ran out and you came in."

"Yeah, I think I heard the door slam," Marshall said. He went over to the door. "The floor is wet here. But the wind could have blown the door open and let some rain in."

"But the person seemed so real," KC said.

"Maybe it was Gus or Anna checking on us," Marshall suggested. "Or your stepdad."

KC shook her head. "They would have said something, not run out the door," she said. "Maybe I did just dream the whole thing."

Marshall walked toward the bedroom. "Or," he added in a deep voice, "it was President Eisenhower taking his little birthday stroll."

"Ha!" KC said. "See you in the morning."

Marshall closed his bedroom door. KC got up and pulled a chair in front of the cabin's front door. She dragged the little chest over and set it on the chair seat. She piled her books on top of the chest.

"Try to get in now," she muttered. Then she shut off the light, curled up on the sofa, and pulled the blanket over her head.

The next morning KC woke up with the sun in her eyes. She lay in the nest of blankets and thought about the night before. She looked at the chair barricade in front of the door and almost laughed.

She sat and stretched. The figure she saw—or thought she saw—must have been part of her dream.

She got up and knocked on Marshall's door. "Are you awake?" she asked.

"What time is it?" came Marshall's voice.

KC checked her watch. "Almost eight. Let's go get breakfast."

They both got dressed and hurried next

door to Aspen. The ground was wet, but the rain and wind had stopped. It looked like a perfect day.

They found Anna in the kitchen. "How did you sleep?" she asked.

KC knew Marshall wanted to say something about the "ghost" last night, but KC spoke first.

"It was great," she said. "Where's my stepdad?"

"He had to leave," Anna said. "He'll be back later. He left you a note in the dining room."

On the table in the dining room, there were two glasses of juice and two place mats. Leaning against one of the juice glasses was an envelope with *KC* written on the front.

KC opened the envelope and pulled out

a slip of paper. She showed it to Marshall.

GOOD MORNING, KIDS.
HAD TO GO BACK TO WHITE
HOUSE. EMERGENCY MEETING.
WILL RETURN BY AFTERNOON
AT LATEST.
ANNA WILL BE AROUND ALL
DAY. ASK GUS TO SHOW YOU THE
BEAVER POND.

LOVE,
DAD

7

What's Under the Floor?

"I wish he had told me he was going," KC said. She slipped the note under her place mat.

"Why?" Marshall asked. He sipped his juice.

KC shrugged. "I don't know, it just feels weird without him here."

Anna came in carrying a tray. "I made scrambled eggs," she said. "Or there's cereal, if you prefer that."

"Eggs are great, thanks," KC said.

Anna set plates of eggs and toast in front of KC and Marshall.

"I have to drive to town for a few lunch things," Anna told them. "I'll be back soon.

Would you like to come with me?"

"No, we'll be fine," KC said.

They heard Anna close the door as she left.

Marshall stuck his fork into his eggs. "Oh, I heard it again," he said.

"Heard what?" KC asked. She nibbled her toast.

"That bumping noise," he said. "You know, under the bathroom floor."

"Is there a basement under our cabin?" KC asked.

"I don't think so," Marshall said. "There's no door to get to it."

"We should ask Anna if she ever heard noises when she was over there," KC said.

"First let's ask Gus to take us to the beaver pond," Marshall said. He had an orange juice mustache.

They finished breakfast and headed outside. Gus was standing next to a truck, talking to another man. A third man was working at a metal box at the top of a telephone pole.

"Don't say anything about last night," KC said.

"Why not?" Marshall asked.

"Because if it was all a dream, I'll feel like a jerk," KC said. "But if there really was someone creeping around in the cabin, it could have been Gus."

The kids walked toward the men. When they got closer, KC read the words THURMONT TELEPHONE on the side of the truck.

"Morning, kids," Gus said when he saw them. "The president had to leave real early, eh? I saw the helicopter take off."

"Yes, but he said he'd be back soon," KC said. "Are they fixing the phones?"

"Yes'm," Gus said. "It's a broken wire. Should be done in a jiffy."

"Can you show us the beaver pond?" Marshall asked. "The president said we should ask you."

"Be happy to," Gus said. "Give me a while to wrap up a few things."

"Let's wait in Aspen," KC said. "Maybe my stepfather will call me when the phone is fixed."

Back inside the lodge, KC found a book and curled up on a sofa. Marshall walked around the room, poking at the walls and bookshelves.

"What're you doing?" KC asked.

"Seeing if I can find the passage your stepdad told us about," he said.

"Marsh, it's supposed to be top secret," KC said.

Marshall wiggled his eyebrows up and down. "That's why I want to find it!"

Just then the telephone rang, making KC jump. She answered it. "Hello, Aspen Lodge. No, she's not working today. She has a cold. Anna is taking her place, but she went shopping."

KC listened for a minute, then hung up.

"Who was that?" Marshall asked. He rapped his knuckles on the side of a bookcase.

"Someone asking for Florence," KC said. "When I said she wasn't here, the guy said he saw her go to work yesterday. She was coming here, Marsh."

"So maybe she got sick after she got

here, then went home," Marshall said. He looked behind a small cabinet.

KC watched Marshall try to find the secret passageway to the tunnel. She thought about everything that had happened since they arrived at Camp David yesterday.

"Come on, Marsh," she said.

"Where are we going?" Marshall asked. "I feel like I'm getting close to the secret door!"

"We're going to find out what's thumping under our cabin," KC said.

"You said it was the pipes," Marshall said.

"That was before weird things started happening around here," KC said. She grabbed Marshall's arm and headed for the door.

"Like what?" Marshall asked.

KC counted off on her fingers. "Like knocking noises under our bathroom floor, windows left open in rainstorms, bats in our cabin, guys creeping around while I'm sleeping . . ."

"I thought you decided that was a dream," Marshall said.

"I changed my mind," KC said.

They crossed the lawn and stepped inside Witch Hazel.

KC went into the bathroom. Marshall followed. They both stood and listened for strange noises.

"Do you hear anything?" KC asked.

Marshall shook his head.

KC ran to the chest and got her flashlight. She came back, kneeled down, and tapped the flashlight on the pipe under the

sink. She waited a few seconds, then tapped again.

"Try turning on the water," Marshall suggested.

KC turned on the water faucet, then turned it off.

Then they heard it. Soft bangs under the floor.

"It's the pipes," Marshall said. "You were right."

KC tapped the pipe with her flashlight three times.

Three taps came back.

KC looked at Marshall. She tapped again, four times.

Four taps came back.

"Do pipes know how to count?" KC asked Marshall.

8
Trapdoor

Marshall stared at KC with huge eyes. "What do you mean?" he asked.

"Marsh, someone is down there!" KC said. "Someone heard me tapping and answered with the same number of taps."

Marshall licked his lips. "Who do you think it is?" he asked. "I mean, what if it's some . . . some swamp monster or something!"

"Yeah, a monster who knows how to count to four," KC said. She ran into the other room and began pushing one end of the sofa.

"What the heck are you doing?" Marshall asked.

"If someone is under our floor, how did they get there?" KC asked. "There must be a hidden door! Help me move this thing!"

KC and Marshall shoved the sofa off the rug. KC lifted the rug and looked underneath. "Not here," she said, flopping the rug back down. "Check all the walls!"

They began tapping on the walls. They found no hollow spots, no strange cracks, nothing that looked like a hidden door.

"Let's check my room," Marshall said.

While Marshall was knocking on the walls, KC pulled his bed away from where it was standing. "It's here!" KC whispered.

In the corner of the room, under the head of Marshall's bed, was a trapdoor. It had been cut into the floor. There was a ring for pulling the door up.

"Oh my gosh!" Marshall croaked. "I was sleeping right on top of it! Something could have reached up and . . . !"

"Marsh, chill and help me open it," KC said.

"Are you nuts?" Marshall asked.

KC raced into the other room. She came back with her Swiss Army knife and handed it to Marshall. "Okay, now let's see what's down there."

She put two fingers inside the ring and pulled. The hinged door came up. KC and Marshall stared into a dark hole. They could see dirt walls on both sides. It smelled damp and felt cold.

"This is what we smelled when we came here yesterday," KC said. "Dirt."

KC shone her flashlight into the hole. A short wooden ladder led down. The floor

was also dirt. KC could see footprints.

"What's that white thing?" Marshall asked. He grabbed KC's hand and aimed the light at a different spot.

"It looks like a food container," KC said. "Like Chinese food."

Marshall giggled. "Do monsters eat Chinese takeout food?"

"I'm going down there," KC said. "You coming?"

"No, I'm getting ready to faint!" Marshall said.

KC shoved her flashlight into her sweatshirt pouch. She sat at the edge of the hole and placed her feet on the top step. "Last chance," she told Marshall.

"Okay! Okay! What do you think, I'm staying up here alone?" he asked.

In a minute, both kids were standing at

the bottom of the hole. It was a dark, damp, and smelly place. KC felt shivers creeping up her spine.

She aimed the light around the walls. "Someone dug this," she said. The dirt was reddish brown, flecked with small stones. The hole was narrow and about five feet deep. KC could touch both walls with her hands. She shivered. It was cold down there.

"I hear something!" Marshall whispered.

KC listened. She heard a sort of humming noise.

She aimed the light beam in front of her. The hole was really the beginning of a tunnel. Seven feet ahead of them, the tunnel turned a corner.

KC walked forward, with Marshall

nearly stepping on her heels. The humming noise grew louder when they went around the bend.

They both saw it at once. At the end of the flashlight beam lay a large white bundle. Rope tied the bundle to a black pipe that ran down the side of the tunnel. The bundle was moving. The humming sound turned into a moan.

"Oh my gosh," gasped Marshall.

KC tilted the flashlight upward. The white bundle had a face and long, dark hair. Its mouth was covered with tape. Wide, frightened eyes stared right at KC and Marshall.

9

A Face at the Window

KC and Marshall ran to the prisoner. On their knees, they began to work on the ropes.

"Wait," Marshall said. He had slipped KC's knife into his pocket. Now he pulled it out and started to cut the rope.

KC peeled the tape from the woman's mouth. She had been wrapped in a sheet. Her arms and legs were also tied.

"Thank you. Thank you," the woman whispered.

In a few moments she was untied. She rubbed her wrists and ankles. "I'm so cold," she said.

"Who are you?" KC asked.

The woman looked at her. "I am Florence," she said. Florence had a long, thin body. Her arms, legs, and gray dress were stained from the red dirt.

"Can you walk?" KC asked. "We can go up to our cabin."

"I think so, but I twisted my ankle when they threw me down here," Florence said. "If you help me, I might be able."

Marshall and KC helped Florence stand on one foot. She had to crouch so her head wouldn't bump the tunnel ceiling. Then they helped her up the ladder. Soon she was lying on Marshall's bed with a blanket wrapped around her shoulders. Marshall replaced the trapdoor.

"I am thirsty," Florence said.

KC ran into the bathroom for a glass of water.

"What happened to you?" Marshall asked.

"Anna and her husband," the woman said. "They put me down there yesterday. They are bad people."

"But Anna told us you were sick," KC said. "She said she was taking your place as housekeeper for the president. He's my stepfather."

"I know. The president has told me about you," Florence said. "But Anna told you lies. They tied me up so they could steal all the good silver from Aspen Lodge! The husband—his name is Casper—he has been digging a tunnel under this cabin all week. The tunnel will connect to the one under Aspen. They planned to take the silver out through this cabin today or tomorrow."

"Marsh, Anna said she went into town," KC said. "She might be back any minute! We can't let her find us!"

"Let's get out of here!" Marshall said. "We have to hide somewhere!"

"I'm sorry," Florence said. "I don't think I can walk very well."

"I have an idea," Marshall said. "Come on!"

They left Florence on the bed and raced to the front room. "Let's move the couch in front of the door," Marshall said.

Each taking one end, they were able to shove the sofa until it blocked the door.

KC pulled down the window shade, then peeked out. "I don't see anyone at Aspen," she said. "But Anna could be back by now. Marsh, we need help. One of us should climb out your bedroom window and go find either Gus or a marine guard."

Marshall gulped. "I'll go," he said. "What if I bump into Anna or her husband?"

"Try to stay hidden," KC said. "But you have to hurry! Anna might come over here looking for us!"

In the bedroom, Florence was sitting up on the bed.

Marshall raised his bedroom window. He and KC looked outside. All they saw were bushes.

Marshall squeezed through the window. He dropped quietly to the ground outside the cabin. He quickly snuck between two bushes and disappeared.

"Good luck," KC whispered. She closed the window and pulled down the shade.

Florence was watching her. "Gus is a

good man," she said. "He will know what to do."

"I wish I could call my stepdad," KC said. She sat on the bed. "But there's no phone in here."

"Where is he?" asked Florence. "I thought he was here, with you."

"He was, but this morning he had to go back to the White House," KC said. "Anna told us at breakfast. He left me a note saying he'd be back this afternoon."

Florence took KC's hand. "Try not to worry," she said.

KC stared at the window through which Marshall had left. If she stared hard enough, maybe she'd see his face, with Gus right behind him.

She looked at the trapdoor. Things were beginning to make sense. Anna's husband was digging a tunnel under this cabin. The dirt she'd seen near Nancy's Walk had been the same red color—had he carried it there? He had to get rid of it somewhere.

Just then KC heard the window being raised. A hand reached in and tugged on the shade, making it roll up.

"Marsh?" KC said.

But the face that suddenly appeared in the window did not belong to her friend. This face had dark eyes rimmed with red. The jaw was covered with black hair. The man wore a hat low on his forehead.

Florence screamed. "It's Casper!" she cried.

Casper looked into the room. When he saw Florence and KC, he turned and ran.

KC raced to the window. She was in

time to see two marines tackle Casper to the ground. One of the men sat on Casper's back. Then KC saw Gus and Marshall run up to the others.

"It's all over, Casper," Gus said.

Marshall looked toward the cabin and saw KC watching from the window. "Cool, huh?" he said with a big grin on his face.

10

Marshall and the Mole People

The president dropped a marshmallow into his hot chocolate. "Gee, I go away for a few hours, and you two break up a ring of thieves," he said. "Your moms will never let me bring you here again."

KC stirred her hot chocolate. "We were just minding our own business," she said. "If Marshall hadn't heard Florence knocking on the pipes, we never would have found her."

"Yeah, and if the phones hadn't gone out, Anna would have been able to warn her husband. And he wouldn't have come into our cabin and scared the heck out of KC," Marshall added.

"We think he kept old clothes and work boots in that little trunk," KC said. "He didn't know Marsh and I were sleeping there, so he came in to do some more digging."

"And I'll bet Anna opened our windows last night," Marshall said. "She hoped bats would fly in and we'd get scared and run over here to Aspen. That way her husband, Casper, could go in and dig."

"It's amazing that he had been digging for over a week and never got caught," the president said. "The FBI discovered that he'd been sleeping in that white laundry van. At night, he'd sneak over to your cabin and dig. Then he'd use a linen cart to haul away the dirt he'd dug up and dump it in the woods."

KC remembered the running figure

she'd seen from the helicopter. That must have been Casper. "So he really did work for the laundry company?" KC asked.

The president nodded. "Yes, and Anna was on the cleaning staff. But when she told him about the silver, Casper got greedy," the president said. "Somehow, she learned that there was a tunnel under Aspen. That's what gave them the idea to dig a new tunnel to remove the silver. By working at night, the security guards would never see them."

"But first they had to get rid of Florence," Marshall added.

"Yes, poor Florence. She would have been in the way when the robbery took place," the president said. "So they hid her in the tunnel under your cabin, thinking no one would ever go there. And Casper could keep an eye on her while he dug."

"Gus said he took her to the hospital," KC said. "I hope she's all right."

"Her ankle had a bad sprain," the president said. "Her family told me she's coming home tomorrow."

"When are we going home?" KC asked her stepfather.

"I thought we'd stay one more night," the president said. "What do you kids think?"

"Great!" KC said. "Gus still needs to show us the beaver pond. And I want to do more exploring!"

"I'll stay only if we can bunk here in Aspen," Marshall said. "I'm not sleeping where people are digging tunnels under my bed!"

The president winked at KC. "Marshall,

did I ever tell you the story about the mole people who live in the sewers under Washington, D.C.?" he asked. "It seems that these giant moles . . ."

Marshall jumped up from the table. He grabbed the bag of marshmallows and ran from the dining room.

Did you know?

Did you know that Camp David was built during the Great Depression? It was a special project for workers who had lost their jobs.

When it opened in 1938, it was called Hi-Catoctin, after the mountain range where it was located. It was a place where government workers could take their families to hike and swim.

In the 1940s, President Franklin D. Roosevelt needed a place to relax outside the city. Normally he would go to the presidential yacht, the USS *Potomac,* but there was a war going on. A boat wasn't safe for the president. He visited a few spots and finally chose Hi-Catoctin. He renamed it Shangri-La. President Eisenhower renamed it again, calling it Camp David after his grandson.

Different presidents used the camp in different ways. President Truman took long walks. President Ford liked to snowmobile on the grounds, while President Carter often went fly-fishing. President Kennedy took his children to visit their ponies. Some presidents—like President George H. W. Bush—went sledding at Camp David with their children.

President Reagan used Camp David the most. He liked horseback riding and did woodworking in his free time. But every president since FDR has gone there to get away from busy Washington, D.C. The president and his family continue to use Camp David to this day!

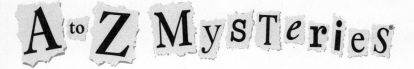

Help Dink, Josh, and Ruth Rose . . .

. . . solve mysteries
from A to Z!

Random House